For Judy and David

All rights reserved. • Published by Schwartz & Wade Books, an imprint of Random House Children's Books, a division of Random House, Inc., New York • Schwartz & Wade Books and the colophon are trademarks of Random House, Inc. • Visit us on the Web! www.randomhouse.com/kids • Educators and librarians, for a variety of teaching tools, visit us at www.randomhouse.com/teachers

Library of Congress Cataloging-in-Publication Data
Russo, Marisabina. • A very big bunny / Marisabina Russo.—1st ed. • p. cm.
Summary: Amelia is so big that she is always last in line at school and none of the other students will play with her, but a special new classmate teaches her that size is not always the most important thing.
ISBN 978-0-375-84463-8 (hc) — ISBN 978-0-375-94463-5 (Gibraltar lib. bdg.)
[1. Size—Fiction. 2. Individuality—Fiction. 3. Schools—Fiction. 4. Friendship—Fiction. 5. Rabbits—Fiction.] I. Title. • PZ7.R9192Ver 2010 • [E]—dc22
2008039924 • The text of this book is set in Stempel Schneidler. • The illustrations are rendered in gouache. • Book design by Rachael Cole

PRINTED IN CHINA
10 9 8 7 6 5 4 3 2 1
First Edition

A VERY BiG BUNNY

MARISABINA RUSSO

schwartz & wade books · new york

Amelia was a bunny.

A very big bunny.

"You really stand out in the crowd," said Mama.
"You're always the star of the show," said Daddy.
But Amelia didn't want to stand out in the crowd
or be the star of the show.
She wanted to be a bunny. A not-so-big bunny.

In school, Amelia was the biggest bunny in her class.

Miss Arugula liked to line up the class in size order.
That's why Amelia was always last.

Going to the gym.

Going to the library.

Going to the cafeteria.

At recess, none of the other bunnies wanted to play with Amelia.

"We can't turn the jump rope high enough for you," said Lavinia.

"Your feet are too big for hopscotch," added Daphne.

And the seesaw was out of the question.

So Amelia stood by the fence and kept herself busy.

Counting the clouds in the sky.
Listening to the wind in the trees.
Thinking about important things.

After school, Amelia walked home by herself.

Along the way she practiced
ballet twirls.

She sang "I'm a Little Teapot."

She picked dandelions
and made herself a crown.

On her walk home, Amelia never felt big.

One day, the door to the classroom opened,
and in walked the principal, Mrs. Radish.
"I would like you to welcome your new
classmate, Susannah," she said.
"What a pip-squeak," whispered Lavinia.
"What a peanut," whispered Justine.
"What a shrimp," whispered Daphne.

Susannah was a bunny.
A very small bunny.

At recess, none of the bunnies wanted to play with Susannah.

"We can't turn the jump rope that low," said Lavinia.

"Your feet are too small for hopscotch," added Daphne.

And the seesaw was out of the question.

Susannah raised her ears as high as they could go and walked over to the fence.

"Hi," she said to Amelia. "What are you doing?"

"Counting the clouds in the sky." Looking down at little Susannah, Amelia felt enormous.

"The clouds are fluffy and puffy today, just like giant cotton candy," said Susannah. "I love cotton candy."

Amelia just kept counting.

"Don't you wish we could hop up to the sky
and ride on the clouds?" said Susannah.
Amelia did not answer.
"Maybe I can help you."
"No, thank you," said Amelia. "I'm a lot closer
to the sky than you are."

The next day at recess, Susannah walked right up to Amelia.

"Hi," said Susannah. "Are you counting the clouds today?"
"No, I'm listening to the wind in the trees," said Amelia.
"If we had umbrellas, we could sail on the wind," said
Susannah. "And fly all around the world, and visit India
and Egypt and China."
"Shhh," said Amelia.
"Can I listen to the wind with you?" asked Susannah.

"I don't think so," said Amelia. "You need really big ears to hear the wind."

And so it went. Every day at recess, Susannah came
over to the fence and asked Amelia what she was doing.

And every day, Amelia had an answer.

"Spelling words that start with a P."

Or "Making dandelion crowns."

Or "Practicing pliés."

But Amelia never invited Susannah to join in.

One afternoon, Miss Arugula announced that picture day
was coming up.

"I expect you all to look your very best!" she added.

"Don't forget to wear one of your dumb dandelion crowns,"
Lavinia whispered to Amelia.

Some of the other bunnies started to laugh.

All the way home, Amelia thought about the class picture. It was very possible that she would have a tummyache or a bad cold on picture day and have to stay home from school.

At recess the next day, Susannah looked different. There was a mysterious bulge under her jacket.

"Meet me on the other side of the playground behind the bench," Susannah whispered to Amelia. "I have a top-secret plan for picture day."

Amelia stared up at the sky. There were no clouds today.

She raised her ears and listened. There was no wind blowing through the trees.

She tried to think of something very important, but nothing came into her head.

With a big bunny sigh, Amelia stood up and followed Susannah across the playground.

Susannah and Amelia sat on the ground behind
the bench. "Dandelion crowns are okay," Susannah
said, "but they droop too fast."

And then Susannah showed Amelia what was
under her jacket.

"We'd better get busy," said Susannah. "We want
to be the stars of the show!"

"We do?" said Amelia.

On picture day, Amelia didn't have a tummyache or a bad cold. She raised her ears as high as they could go and put on her favorite dress, her purple tights, and her party shoes.

Susannah was waiting for Amelia by the schoolyard.
The two bunnies finished getting ready for the class
picture. Then they hurried into school.

"Oh, my!" said Miss Arugula.

"I don't think you're allowed to wear tiaras for the class picture," said Lavinia.

"Tiaras are fine," said Miss Arugula. "And quite original."

Amelia was a very big bunny and Susannah was very small,
but from then on, it didn't seem to matter.

Together they counted the clouds in the sky and listened to
the wind in the trees.

They made jewelry and practiced spelling words.

They twirled and sang, and one day they even discovered . . .

that the seesaw was not out of the question.